SURF GECKO
TO THE
RESCUE!

WRITTEN & ILLUSTRATED BY
BRUCE HALE

For Mom and Dad, who read me stories
and taught me to love nature.

Also by Bruce Hale:

Legend of the Laughing Gecko

The Adventures of Space Gecko

A major "mahalo" to Marie Reiko Miyashiro and Brian Reed for their assistance,
and to Janette for inspiration and support.

Library of Congress Catalog Card Number: 91-71944
ISBN: 0-9621280-1-5

First printing: October 1991
Second printing: November 1994

Printed in Hong Kong.

B etter than anything in the world, Moki the Gecko loved to surf. Every day, he'd ride the sparkling blue waves at Secret Beach with his best friend, Rudi Mynah Bird. Moki was the best surfer among all the animals and Rudi, even though she was a bird, ran a close second.

When Moki and Rudi were all surfed out, they'd sit in the shade of the coconut trees, listening to Oldturtle's stories. Nobody knew just

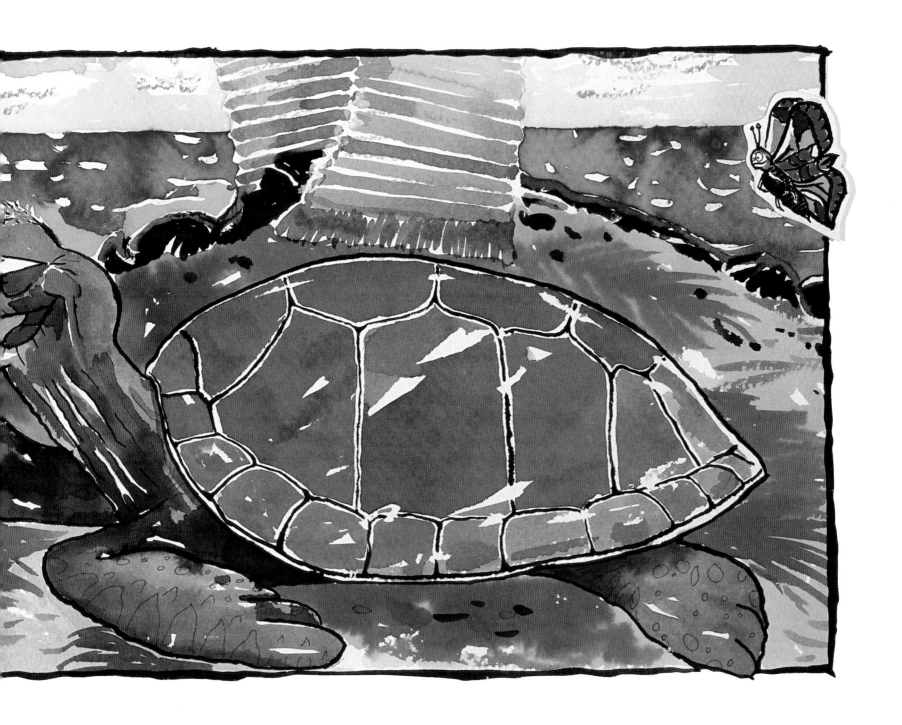

how old Oldturtle was. But one thing was certain: he told the best
stories of anybody around.

Oldturtle also warned Moki and Rudi about humans. "Sometimes, they're as headstrong as wild boars," he said. "They don't know their own strength and they've forgotten how to take care of the land. We have to help them."

"Awk, awk!" squawked Rudi. "Since when have they ever listened to us animals? We can't do a thing."

Oldturtle bobbed his head wisely: "Mark my words, young bird. One day, all the humans will wake up and take notice."

O ne glorious day in late summer, Moki and Rudi came to Secret
Beach and found it wasn't so secret anymore. Up and down
the golden sands were scattered dirty papers and empty soda cans.
Trash floated in the sparkling blue water.

"Oh no!" cried Moki. "What happened to our beautiful beach?"

"Let's find Oldturtle. He'll tell us," Rudi said.

Rudi's sharp eyes spotted the turtle out on the reef. She and Moki almost burned up the water, paddling out on Moki's surfboard.

When they reached him, Oldturtle was gasping for breath, half in and half out of the water. His head and front legs were tangled in some strange, clear material which choked his throat as he struggled.

"Hold still! We'll get you out of it!" cried Moki.

He and Rudi tried pulling at the clear thing, but it was wrapped too tightly. Then, snip-snip, Rudi cut the plastic with her sharp beak.

"Well, bless my tailfeathers, what happened here?" she asked.

"Many humans," croaked Oldturtle. "They came and ate on the beach. They left this awful mess."

The three animals swam to the beach while Oldturtle told his story.

"As I came up out of the water to ask them to clean it up, I got caught in one of these," he said, kicking another plastic thing with his foot. "If you hadn't showed up, I might have died."

When he heard that, Moki's worry turned to anger. He slapped his tail on the sand.

"How dare they!" he cried. "Those stupid humans trashed our favorite beach and I'm not going to stand for it!"

"Awk! Me neither," squawked Rudi. "Let's take this trash and dump it right back in the humans' city. We'll see how they like it!"

Oldturtle held up a wrinkled flipper: " Don't get your belly in a bumpus and act from anger — that's not the way to teach. If you litter the humans' city, you're as bad as they are.

"Besides, they might not notice it."

Moki's tail lashed the sand like a crazy snake. "But what can we do?" he cried. "I won't just sit here and let them ruin this beach."

Oldturtle sat silent as a stone, thinking. Moki and Rudi paced beside him until they wore ruts into the sand.

Finally, Oldturtle smiled.

"There is a way," he said, "to make the humans listen. Tell me, Moki, Rudi — just how good is your surfing?"

The next day, Moki, Rudi and Oldturtle went to another beach, one where many humans surfed and played in the waves. Oldturtle pointed to a sign and read it out loud.

"It says, 'Big Surf Contest today. Winner gets $10,000,'" the turtle said. "You two are going to enter this contest. If you win, I guarantee everyone will listen to you."

Moki looked around. Many of the world's best surfers had come, from Killer Kimo and Radical Remo to Goofy Foot Georgie. How could a little gecko and a mynah bird beat such champions? Moki bit his lip. Rudi hopped nervously from foot to foot. For their beach, they had to win.

The starting horn blew. When Moki caught that first wave and danced across its face on his little board, the contest judges couldn't believe their eyes.

"Get that little kid out of there!" said one.

"Hey, that's no kid, that's a surfing gecko," said the head judge.

"And a darned good one, too," the third judge said. "Let's send him to the next round."

Then Rudi caught her first wave.

"What's that? A feather duster?" said the first judge.

"No, sir, it's a mynah bird. And she looks good, too," said another.

"Now I've seen everything," sighed the head judge. "A surf bird and a surf gecko. What's next, a surf elephant?"

The long day wore on. Moki and Rudi were good, but so were the other surfers. Then, Rudi took off late on one big wave and it slammed her board to the bottom. Snap! -- it broke in half like a popsicle stick. Holy Majoley! Shaken but still in one piece, the bird swam to shore. It was all up to Moki now.

Finally, it came down to the last three surfers: Killer Kimo, Radical Remo and Moki the Gecko.

Remo went first. He surfed well, he surfed wonderfully, but in the end he fell off his board. Radical Remo was out.

Killer Kimo caught the next wave. He rode his board like a wild horse, bucking and spinning, pulling tricks never seen before. The judges were impressed.

"Hmph!" said the head judge. "Let's see the surf gecko beat that."

Moki waited for the right wave. Then it came — a huge wall of blue water, the biggest wave of the day. Moki looked down and took the drop.

It was like he'd jumped from a rooftop and now the house was

chasing him. Up, down, back and forth across the monster wave's face Moki rode, surfing with all his might. He did handstands, tailstands, and even carved his name on the blue water.

But would the judges like him better than Killer Kimo?

The contest judges huddled. They whispered together for a long time while everyone waited breathlessly. At last, the head judge turned to the crowd and cleared his throat.

"Ladies and gentlemen...and animals," he said. "We declare the winner of this contest to be: The surf gecko!"

Moki bounced up and down on the tip of his tail, he was so happy. Oldturtle and Rudi beamed.

The happy crowd shouted, "Speech! Speech!" as Moki jumped up onto the judges' table and raised his hands for quiet.

"My name is Moki," he told the people. "And I don't want your prize money, I want your attention.

"I won this contest for the beaches and my fellow animals, not for myself. Listen, something bad is happening to our beaches."

Moki told them about the garbage on Secret Beach and how it almost killed Oldturtle. When he finished, the people were silent, ashamed.

"But what can we do?" asked Goofy Foot Georgie at last.

"Stop littering the beaches," said Moki. "And if you see trash there already, pick it up. The beaches are there for all of us — human and animal."

Everyone promised to work harder at keeping the beaches clean. And they acted on their promise by picking up trash all over the beach where the contest was held. Radical Remo even vowed to start a clean-up campaign with Moki's prize money.

"Hooray for Moki the Surf Gecko!" the crowd shouted.

It was almost dark when Oldturtle and Rudi left a tired, happy surf gecko at his own front door. Moki hugged his friends, then asked Oldturtle: "Do you really think the humans will keep their promise?"

"For our sake and theirs, I hope so," Oldturtle said. "And if they forget, we'll just remind them again. Sometimes you have to work to make a change."

Inside the gecko home, Moki's mother was cooking dinner.
"Did you have a good day, dear?" she asked.
"Like you wouldn't believe, Mom," said Moki. "I'm starving.
When's dinner?"

Moki's mother put her hands on her hips. "No dinner for you
until you clean up your room, Mr. Surf Gecko," she said.
    "But Mom..."

Moki looked at the mess in his room and sighed. He thought about the trash on the beach.

And he reached down, and started picking up his toys.